The Pi

By Kathy LaFollett

Musings of the Day series
Volume 1
Volume 2
Volume 3
Volume 4
Volume 5 (expected release Fall 2021)

High Ceilings - Musings of a Childhood (expected release Fall 2021)

Jack Crow Trilogy
Jack Crow Knows
Forget What you Think you Know Jack Crow
(expected release Spring 2022)
What do you know, Jack Crow? (expected release Spring 2023)

The Art of the FlockCall - Your Successful Companion Parrot Lifestyle

Dear Felix Diary Thingy - Felix in the Time of Confused

Directions for the Confused - How to Think Like a Parrot

Detective Felix Series
Book 1 - *The Pistachio Alley Puzzle*
Book 2 – *The Exploding Phonebook Factory Caper*
(expected release Winter 2021)

CHILDREN'S TITLES

How Do you Do? Very Well, Thank You!

Oh, but Grandma Loves You!

Little Sea Piggles

The Pistachio Alley Puzzle | A Detective Felix Mystery

Detective Felix Mystery Stories
The Pistachio Alley Puzzle

...but nobody asks the Felix.
Felix LaFollett, detective

...it's nobody's business at all.
Leonidas Rabbit, FBI, retired

This book is a work of fiction. Names, characters, places, and incidents are the product of the author's imagination, conjuring, and used fictitiously if not playfully. Any resemblance to actual events, locales, or persons living or dead, is coincidentally confused. Furthermore, I baked this cake myself.

Copyright © 2021 by Kathy LaFollett | Reciprocity Productions LLC

ISBN: 9798716726710
First Edition 2021
Reciprocity Productions LLC

The scanning, uploading, and distribution of this book without permission is a theft of the author's intellectual property. If you would like permission to use material from this book (other than review purposes), please contact the author directly through her website flockcall.com. Thank you for your support of the author's rights.

Author is available for speaking engagements virtual or live via Reciprocity Productions. Contact the author directly for availability. Felix is available virtually. Felix does not fly. On planes. That would be ridiculous.

Chapter One – *Shell Shocking Clues!*

The pistachio shells left clues. The alleyway was a war zone of pistachio hand grenade explosions. If pistachios were grenades. But they are not. Who would throw all these shells all over the alley? And where were the pistachio's insides? The crime scene lay out in front of Detective Felix like a worm blanket. Filled with all the thingys that are wrong, and no good reason why they were there. It was up to Detective Felix to find that reason, decide if it was good, and then after that he will find the criminal and end his criminaling activities.

Detective Felix heard talons of fury steps behind him. He heard them fly in before they started toward him. The Foragensics Team was ready to gather the evidences. He turned to see his team approaching. "Morning, Snickers. It's ugly."

Snickers had his rubber talon gloves already on and ready to pick up disgusting evidences. "Yeah, boss. We heard. Pistachio homicides are the ugliest."

Detective Felix looked down at a pistachio shell all alone farthest away from the scene. He looked up at Snickers in his rubber talon gloves. "Snickers, I'm not sure if this wasn't a kidnapping. Better follow the evidences."

"You got it, boss."

Detective Felix walked past Snickers and stood next to Butters. She was the best in the businesses in getting photographical evidences no matter how much confused there was.

"Morning, Boss. Snickers was pretty excited about a homicide job. You know he likes going through messes."

"Butters." Detective Felix nodded a greeting while he watched Snickers forage for the evidences. "How was your vacation?"

"Tasty. It's pomegranate season you know."

The Pistachio Alley Puzzle | A Detective Felix Mystery

Detective Felix chewed on a straw he pulled out of his Detective Pocket. "Pomegranate season ..." He spoke the words not intending to join a conversation, but rather, consider the evidences and the work ahead of them while rolling words around in his mouth and head. Word tumbling helped his thinking.

"Make sure to get the pictures of all the pistachio shells and alsotoo, take the pictures of all the garbage cans around the here. And Butters ..." Detective Felix looked up into the trees overhanging the alleyway. The entire length of the alley on this block was shaded by large old trees and their overhanging branches. He squinted hard to see what may lay inside the foliage. "Butters, if you see any twitchy squirrels take their pictures."

"Okay, boss." Butters looked up following the gaze of the best detective she ever worked with in her career fighting criminaling activities. Detective Felix seemed to see everything at once. Her work was never wasted on The Felix.

Detective Felix turned to walk out of the alley and to his Detective Office of Investigationings.

"Psssst!" The sound came from the left side of the alley.

Detective Felix paused walking to look left to see a foot protruding from behind an old mattress that leaned against a shed that leaned against a tree. If it weren't for the tree, everything would fall down. A paw revealed itself while grabbing the edge of the mattress with it's black and grey furry fingers. Then a snout with whiskers askew, reached back to two black glassy eyes surrounded by a mask of black fur. The glassy eyes were circled by grey eyelashes.

"Pssst!"

"I'm here. I heard your *pssst* the first time." Detective Felix always found the cloaking and the daggering annoying. Get to the points. The points were easy to get to.

The Pistachio Alley Puzzle | A Detective Felix Mystery

"Hey, detective. I got some information you might want." The snout led to a full head of raccoon named Clyde. "I was in the garbage cans when I heard something."

"You are always in the garbage cans. That's what you do." Detective Felix and his raccoon snitch had been working together for years. It was Clyde's information that helped solve The Precarious Picnic Basket on the Roof Case. It was Clyde who put it there. Which turned the case into a mistake, rather than a crime.

"Maybe I'm in garbage cans all the time, but I did hear something weirdo. It could be a clue. If …you know …you have something for me."

Detective Felix reached into his Detective Pocket, he pushed aside his extra straws, dug under his extra spatula, pushed aside his lucky purple plastic rocking horse, and found Clyde's bribe. A strawberry. He pulled it out and tossed it underwing to Clyde who grabbed it out of the air like an eager baseball catcher during spring training.

"Talk." Detective Felix was getting the hangries and was ready for lunch.

"Well, I was over there, the next garbage cans over. Yesterday was Wednesday. They always get take outs on Tuesday night. They had gyros last night. So I'm eating and I'm down in the can, so you know I can't see anything, but I can hear things, right? And I hear voices and footsteps. And they stop right by my can and I'm thinkin', I'm pinched!"

"That is not information, Clyde. That is blah-blahs."

"Right, right. So I hear one voice say, *What's the point of flying out on Thursday? What's the rush?* And he's eating something right? His words are all crunchy and chewing around the edges. And then the other voice says, *What are you talking about! I booked these flights months ago! I'm not cancelling flights because you want to sleep in, this was your idea!*" Clyde took a bite of his payment.

The Pistachio Alley Puzzle | A Detective Felix Mystery

"Is there information in all the blah-blahs, Clyde, because you are already eating that strawberry." Detective Felix was on his last nerve ending. Nobody could get The Felix on his last nerve ending like Clyde.

"Right. Yayaya! So, the first voice says, *Fine! Maybe one day you'll explain to me why you always book flights for the morning. Because no one else does that.* And the second voice says, *Everyone else is not a vampire, Todd.* Clyde delivered that last line slowly, elongating the words for presentation and clarity. He held the strawberry in both paws now, just below his mouth. His eyes were wide with punctuated excitement. Expectation was written all over his whiskers. "VAMPIRES." He whispered the word with a menacing hiss.

"Vampires." Detective Felix spoke the word to make sure this is where all those blah-blahs took him. He pulled the collar of his Detective Coat up. To keep The Confused from sliding in behind his coat. So much Confused.

"VAMPIRES." Clyde nodded his head and took another bite between knowing nods. His confidence growing with each new nod. He turned and walked back behind the mattress to finish his strawberry, with every step whispered "vampires" as if in a trance. The strawberry juice left behind red stains, that left Clyde looking like a vampire as he took one final look back to Detective Felix. His canine fang and grin delivering the sweet look of ridiculous with a whispered promise of *...v a m p i r e s ...*

Detective Felix pulled a new straw from his Detective Pocket and stuck it in his beak. He chewed on the end taking in the information. He knew one new thing to know. Two were eating in the alley last night. Clyde and a vampire.

"Pffft!" Detective Felix let his opinion out like steam from a tea kettle and headed toward his investigationings office. "Vampires. Pffft!"

Chapter Two - *Fast Through Pass Through*

Detective Felix put on his Detective Coat. He dropped his extra spatula, chew straws, one walnut, three pasta wheelies, one strawberry for bribes, his Detective Notebook for Notes of Thinking, along with The Pen into his Detective Coat Pocket. It was time for breakfast before it was time for investigationings. You can't think on an empty stomach. Alsotoo, who would want to?

Felix found his favorite seat at the Fast Through Pass Through Diner. This time of morning the sun was shining too bright to be on the other side. Here he sat in the shadows, getting his detective thinkings going.

The Fast Through Pass Through Diner wasn't the best in town. Service was slow. The second cook was confused, and he most likely would be sending his bowl back to the kitchen for fixing. But Leonidas owned the place. That rabbit made up for all the down fallings.

"Morning, Detective. The usual?" His waitress. Not awake yet.

"I want some apple popcorn." Detective Felix sipped the tea that was ready and waiting, thanks to Marie.

"You got it. The usual plus sides. Any good cases today?"

"Just one. You probably won't be interested unless you like raccoons who see vampires walking on empty pistachio shells."

Marie laughed, snapping her chewing gum between her molars. She stuck her pencil behind her ear and turned to get Detective Felix's order hung on the spindle. Detective Felix was one of the best, and she was glad to be his waitress.

Felix stopped her progress with a question. "Is Leonidas back there?"

She answered over her shoulder still heading to the kitchen. "Always is ...LEO! The Detective is asking for you!" The double doors swung wildly with a puff of air and friction as she entered the kitchen, revealing the inner workings of The Pass Through Fast Through Diner. As the doors swung out again, He caught sight of two long ears near the flattop, and four ground squirrels chopping, stirring, and prepping for the two long ears near the flattop.

He sipped his warm tea. Marie always knew to have the tea waiting. Peach tea, warm enough to sip but not cool enough to gulp.

Leonidas appeared from the doors that Marie disappeared behind. He was wiping his paws on a chef's towel that had seen better days. He had a green bean hanging from his mouth. Something he'd done his entire cooking career. Which was two seasons. Unlike his FBI career that was eleven seasons. They say that an oral fixation like a green bean keeps the mind steady while concentrating. Others say it's a way to hide feelings. Leonidas believed it was nobody's business why he chewed on a green bean all day. Nobody's business at all.

"Morning, Felix." Leonidas was one of the few that didn't bother with the label of detective. An unwritten code between the FBI Agent (retired), and the Detective.

"Morning, Leonidas. What's cooking?" They grinned at each other as two friends do after having known each other this long. Banter being personal signs of a long friendship.

Leonidas set the loosely folded chef towel down on top of the ice chest behind the counter. Leaned one paw near the pie display. "Nothing you'd want to eat. What's the case this time?" Leo adjusted his green bean to the left side of his mouth for listening.

Leo and Felix worked out cases together. It started with that basket on a roof incident after Leonidas had retired. He appreciated Felix bringing in mysteries and crime solutions not yet solved. Being retired FBI, owning a diner was not what Leonidas had pictured when he was a young bun. He bought The Fast Through Pass Through Diner before thinking all the way through, which rabbits tend to do. No point in selling and getting a Private Investigation Bunny License now. He could have his carrot cake and eat it too, thanks to Felix.

"It's a case right up your alley, in a alley. There's vampires. According to Clyde anyway." Felix sipped his warm tea.

Marie's voice called out from the kitchen. "When you two are done playing Sherlock Holmes and Dr. Watson out there, I've got a spindle full of orders hanging in here, Leonidas! Including yours Detective! Somebunny want to cook today? Any detectives want to eat? Just asking!"

Leonidas pulled the green bean from his mouth, and threw back the usual retort. "Thanks for the update, Marie! Gary, you're on the flat top!"

The hustle and bustle of ground squirrel shouts took over the kitchen as his crew shifted to take Leonidas' place.

Sticking the green bean back into his mouth he looked at Detective Felix. Delivering the stealthy grin of a rabbit hungry for a mystery. "Do tell, Mr. Holmes, do tell." Leo leaned in to listen.

Chapter Three - *Fourth Street North*

As Marie set Felix's usual order plus sides down on the counter, a widower one block north of the crime scene woke to the sound of barking squirrels ready for their usual morning fare.

Jake lost his wife a handful of years before. They had lived in the house on Fourth Street their entire marriage. It was a good house. Theirs was a better marriage. He missed her still, and fed her collection of wild squirrels and birds as he had promised her the day she said good-bye.

He'd not moved a thing since he came home that first day alone. No point in it. Everything was where he liked it, as she had liked it, too. A small one bedroom cracker box home it had its own one car garage that emptied onto the alley behind. They had stopped driving a year before she left. Their four-door sat idle all these years inside. His son had offered to take it. He declined. He and Sandra had shared too many trips, too many conversations, and far too many laughs to let the car go.

Jake walked out onto his cement front steps grabbing the wrought iron handrail to steady himself. Sandra's squirrels were impatient. Scattered throughout the oak tree overhead, the ground below, and one very opinionated squirrel stationed on the roof overhanging the porch itself. He barked demands, more squeaky than sharp.

Jake sat down on the second to the last step from the sidewalk. "Alright, alright ...come and get your peanuts." His eyes focusing in the new light of outdoor sunshine. He waited and watched the gathering surround him at his feet. Claws skittered on rooftop, tree bark, and cement. His wife's horde of twitching tails prepared their paws to receive breakfast.

His eyes' focus grew as his iris adjusted to the new light. Jake took in his breakfast customers, and his yard. "What's this? Did you bring all this here? I just swept!"

Jake didn't mind wildlife, didn't mind the squirrels. Didn't mind filling Sandra's birdfeeder. He fed the squirrels nuts without shells for a reason, though. Sweeping sidewalks wasn't a chore his hands or hips liked much anymore. He only just this year started paying the neighbor kid to mow his front lawn. What there was of it.

He leaned over and picked up a pistachio shell. He looked out over the sidewalk and his just mowed lawn and saw more. Empty pistachio shells with no reason to be there. He looked over his shoulder following the trail of shells to the alley.

"Hnh. Seems somebody with money has decided to feed you freeloaders!" Jake, laughed and tossed peanuts, one each, at the feet of each squirrel Sandra had loved immensely. "Look here, do me a favor and leave those shells in the yard you found them. He tossed two peanuts at the feet of his roof barker. Being the biggest and in charge of the clan, he was the most vocal with Jake. He barked a raspy squirrel retort, rubbing his paws together. Jake would take this as an accord for now.

"I'll get all the evidences Butters and Snickers gathered today. In the meantime, I've only interviewed Clyde. It cost me a whole strawberry to hear about Vampires." Felix had finished his breakfast order, and was sipping his warm tea.

Leonidas had joined him on the stool next over while Detective Felix told him all he knew at this point about the Pistachio Alley Incident. Leonidas took a long drink of carrot juice. "I'm guessing vampires are not on your short list of perps."

Felix laughed a healthy chuckle. "No, but Clyde is on my short nerve ending."

"I'd be interested in seeing all the details Snickers and Butters put together." Leonidas had left the FBI (Furry Bureau of Investigationings) just a few years before. Retired with a good pension. He liked cooking and bought the diner on a future fluke investment. A rabbit needs to keep his mind sharp. And a rabbit needs a healthy supply of carrot juice. All in all, considering an alternative of sleeping his rabbit life away in a warren somewhere, it seemed to work out.

"Stop by the Tree Tent Office today after you close up. We can go over things. Right now I just have the one question, where's the body?"

Leonidas thumped in agreement. "You've got a bagful of pistachio bodies to start!"

Detective Felix's Cellphone fartsounded. He had a text.

"The Whoa. Looks like we have another crime scene. On the same street, same alley way ...one block north."

"Sounds like your criminal has decided to take his or her show on the road." Leonidas finished his carrot juice. Heading back to the kitchen he tipped an ear to his friend, "Let me know when you're back and ready to look at all the evidences that foragensics gathered."

Detective Felix nodded as he put his coat back on, pulling up the collar to make sure no confused slipped in. Leonida's kitchen doors swung closed as Felix stepped out the Fast Through Pass Through Diner's front door, into the sun. His eyes worked hard to focus. His detective skills were already sharp.

Chapter Four - *Digesting the Crime*

Detective Felix met Foragensics Team Butters and Snickers at the second crime scene. Both were busy, Butters taking photos of the strewn empty shells, and Snickers gathering evidences inserting them into Evidence Bags for Looking At. Detective Felix found the witness patting Angus on the head under a tree, next to the alley.

"K9 Angus! Aren't you supposed to be on the scent, finding a trail?" Detective Felix didn't want appearances of preferential treatments or treats at a criminaling scene. It could come back to snorfle them in the butt at trial.

"Oh! Yes! Sure, boss. I was just about to find a trail when this guy came out and said I was a good boy. And good looking!" Angus' tail was wagging at a ridiculous rate. "This guy is a really nice guy!"

"K9 Angus, go lay down. Get your head on straight and get on that trail." He spoke to Angus, but looked at the witness with a shrug.

"Okay, boss. I'm on it! After I lay down." Angus dropped under the tree and panted. Waiting for his heartbeat to slow down so he could smell again. Hound brains wobble. Their noses work all the time, but their brains easily loose track of what the nose is doing. Because hound brains are wobbly. A hound has to lay down, slow down, and rebound. K9 Angus' brain was very, very wobbly.

Detective Felix pulled out his Detective Notebook of Notes for Thinking from his Detective Pocket, and The Pen at the ready.

"Hello."

"Good Morning, Detective."

"Can you walk me through what happened here?"

"Yes, sir. I can. Darndest thing really ..." Jake walked Detective Felix through the incident. He also gave him the name of his

The Pistachio Alley Puzzle | A Detective Felix Mystery

lawnmower neighborling kid. In case he knew something or saw something. Felix wrote all the evidences down for later digesting. "Thank you, sir. You've been very helpful."

"You're welcome, Detective. I sure hope you find the culprit. This is a nice neighborhood. We don't have any weirdos at all. I'd like it to stay that way."

"Wouldn't we all, sir. Wouldn't we all." With that Detective Felix flipped his Detective Notebook closed and stowed The Pen with it inside his Detective Pocket. He felt a new straw behind it. Felix brought out his straw and put it in the side of his beak. It really helped thinking.

The witness stepped back into his house with soft slap of his wooden screen door. A screen door that had a gash in the screen. Could be something, could not be something. Felix made a mental note to go down the alley and check all the screen doors of all the houses on this alley. It's the little thingys.

K9 Angus ran up to the Detective. "Boss! You are not going to believe what I found!"

Detective Felix chewed his straw, "Try me."

"A raccoon! And he says it's VAMPIRES!" K9 Angus was a good dog. Exciteabled, but good. He really wanted to be a good boy. He really had a wobbly brain.

"Did you smell a vampire in the vicinity?" Felix cocked his head and narrowed his Eye of Thinking.

"Um. No." K9 Angus' tail slowed it's helicopter spin just a little.

"Did you SEE a vampire?"

"No ...not yet ..." K9 Angus' tail swayed slowly back and forth. The white tip trailing the black end with every swish. His eyes softened.

"Good job, K9 Angus! We've eliminated Vampires thanks to you! They can't be a criminaling element because you didn't see or smell them! Good boy!" Detective Felix removed the straw from his beak and patted Angus on the head.

Angus' tail started spinning so fast it didn't look like a tail anymore, but a helicopter in flight. His brain went wobble. "I'm a GOOD BOY! Right Detective?"

"Yes, you are, K9 Angus! Now, go get me criminal scent trails to track!"

With that Angus burst from sitting tall into forward motion like a rocket. Heading in the wrong direction. Because he didn't reboot his wobbly brain first.

Detective Felix had a soft spot for dogheads that tried. He shook his head, pulled up his Detective Coat collar so the confused didn't get in, adjusted his straw, and headed back to his digesting perch to think on all he'd written down. Hopefully his Foragensics Team left all their evidences there. He had a lot to digest. Hopefully Leonidas brought tea. He was thirsty.

At least the vampire thingy was settled.

K9 Angus sped past Detective Felix as that last thought spun through his mind. Angus turned to look and nod to Felix. Angus' tongue hung out fully, drooling, wagging in the wind.

At least the vampire thingy was settled, maybe.

Detective Felix headed toward his Tree Tent Office to meet Leo. He heard the herculean efforts of a hound in full zoomie mode behind him. It would take the rest of the day for K9 Angus' brain to un-wobble after that. Felix sighed a grin.

At least the vampire thingy was settled, maybe. But probably not from the sounds of Angus' puffing and panting.

Chapter Five - *Lunch with the FBI*

Detective Felix headed back to his Detective Tree Tent, thinking about vampires and Clyde. Only Clyde would be that proud of that much ridiculous. K9 Angus was adding his spin to that ridiculous with one good sniff, and a zoomie. The Detective stopped at the end of the alley between both crime scenes to pull out his Detective Notebook of Notes for Thinking, to make a thinking note.

Do not talk to Clyde. He printed the letters clearly. He circled the note three times for importance and remembering. He underlined all that, once. And doodled a picture of a raccoon with a confused face. Drew an arrow from the note to the Universal Doodle for Confused Raccoon.

He paused putting The Pen to his beak in thought then notated, *Probably a weirdo.* Drew a doodle of the letter W with one eyeball doodle in each V of the W. Then a hangy tongue from the middle upside down ^ at the bottom of the W. The Universal Doodle for Weirdo. He added an arrow from the Universal Doodle for Weirdo back to the Universal Doodle for Confused Raccoon, then flipped his notebook closed.

"Phffffftt." A longer than normal dismissive raspberry fart escaped his beak unconsciously. Keeping weirdos straight took up too much time.

A rustled branch above interrupted the detective's thoughts. "Hey, parrot."

"Detective." Felix looked up to find Jack, perched in the oak. "Detective and you know it."

"Sure. Hey, I just got back from lunch at the Fast Through Pass Through. Leo was telling me about your crime scenes, vampires, missing bodies, and evidence. He also told me you talked to Clyde."

Detective Felix met Jack a handful of seasons before, in the Spring. The time when the ducks started showing up for breakfast and dinner service at his place. *She* seemed intent on feeding the entire universe's worth of ducks. And there was no stopping her. He let it slide in the beginning, she kept serving his meals first, before the barbarian hordes of ducks. It's hard to get good help. Then spring came, and Jack, and more ducks and gull, and Jack's murder, and that one duck, Morty, who really was a dick. Not a dick as in detective, but, a dick as in jerk.

Jack was a talker, and he favored *her*. It's hard to get good help. Detective Felix appreciated her. Didn't mind it when she called herself "mom", and him "birdie". Didn't mind her doting and singing at bedtime. Because it is really very hard to find good help these days. Jack's favoring her brought local gossip, news, and insights of the area to Detective Felix. Jack offered up all the information for nothing. *She* was already paying him with peanut butter crackers and grapes. Felix didn't need to do anything more than offer company and an ear to listen. Crows are talkers.

"Glad to hear Leonidas has tight lips. It's a wonder he's still not in the FBI. Did he happen to say anything about meeting me at my office?"

The undoing was the introduction of Jack to Leonidas. Two talkers in the same circle of information can get hairy.

"My lips are sealed, Detective. But you should probably know a thing I know about a truck, two boxes, a skateboard, and a lawnmower. And I didn't ask him about his plans. He's a grown rabbit!"

"No vampires?" Felix George Bush chuckled pulling out a new Thinking Straw. He stuck the end in his beak, and dropped The Pen where he'd found the straw.

"I'd suggest you stop talking to Clyde, Detective. But I can keep a murder's worth of eyes out for vampires. If you like." Jack cackled a crow laugh that bounced off the leaves and sheds surrounding them leaving a soft echo in its place.

The Pistachio Alley Puzzle | A Detective Felix Mystery

"I think, Jack Crow, I'd like to hear that lawnmower, skateboard, two boxes, and a truck story." Detective Felix leaned against a blue bucket filled with rain water and leaves.

Felix pulled out his Detective Cellphone of Communicationing and texted Leonidas. MET JACK AT CRIME SCENE. MEET YOU AT THE FAST THROUGH LATER. JACK HAS INFORMATION.

His cellphone fartsounded back with a responding Leo text. NO HE DOESN'T. HE HAS WORDS IN THE WRONG ORDER.

Felix texted four laughing emoji and one face palm emoji. Then dropped his phone into his Detective Pocket.

Jack jumped to the brim of the bucket to have a beak to beak conversation. "The entire scene was weirdo, Detective."

"Isn't it always, Jack?"

Chapter Six - *A Long Story Short*

The thing about stories is they have to be told in a straight line for the storyteller to keep it all straight. The thing about life is, there are no straight lines going anywhere. This is why not all are cut out to be a detective. Not everyone can take in straight lines, knot them correctly to create reality for review, while ending up with the conclusion the criminal never wanted on display.

Detective Felix was born to detective.

"Start from the beginning, Jack." Felix leaned against the blue bucket holding his Detective Notebook of Notes for Thinking in one wing, and The Pen in his other. His Thinking Straw hung from his beak while he chewed thoughts. He readied himself to write down the straight lines that needed knotting.

"It starts at your first witness front yard. The murder and I were waiting on his roof to see if the family on the other side of the street were going to fill the birdfeeder. Then we wait for the blue jays to throw everything out. Then we wait for the squirrels to knock it down. Then we eat. It takes about twenty minutes." Jack dipped into the bucket for a drink. He had a long straight line to draw. "The boy was mowing your witness yard then. The lawn had grown longer than usual, because of the rain and his cold. He's mowing long grass that's wet from the night before. Remember all the morning fog that day?"

"Yes, yes I do, Jack." Felix wrote down, *wet grass, front yard, kid had a cold before, foggy morning.* The trick to finding straight lines that need knots is writing down all the words that are possible. None of the words that talk about straight lines that go nowhere. And remembering the best clues are on the edge between those two. "It's getting warmer, everything is starting to spring up, including trouble." He didn't write his own words down.

"The kid's mowing and Jake comes out on the front porch and asks him if he needs a rest or a drink, since he just got over that cold. The kid says no thank you. That he wants to finish and he's okay. About that time the neighbor started filling her birdfeeder, my murder left me for their roof. So the rest I can't corroborate."

The Pistachio Alley Puzzle | A Detective Felix Mystery

"That's okay. You've never given me information that proved wrong." Detective Felix wrote down, *neighbor birdfeeder filling, murder flew off.* Not that anyone in Jack's murder would carry out criminaling activities. But a good detective writes down the names that are cleared as well as the names that are not.

"About that time, the boy is finishing up, and one of his friends shows up on a skateboard. She's got two boxes. They talk."

Felix writes down, *finished mowing, girl with two boxes arrives.* "Did you hear what they said to each other?" He looks up at Jack with the question.

"Some of it. She asked if he was feeling better. He said yes. She said he missed the math test and it was hard. He said he'd heard. He asked her what was in the boxes. She was about to answer but then the boy started swatting his legs and said, "Man these things are vampires!" She laughed. And told him he should have worn long pants and not shorts."

Felix stopped writing, pulling his straw from his beak with the wing holding The Pen. "Vampires? Did you see any vampires? You know Clyde mentioned them before."

"Yeah. I didn't see any. But then again, I wouldn't know what a vampire looks like to look at."

"Did you see Clyde there?"

"No. But you know raccoons, if they don't want to be seen, you aren't going to see them. I suppose he could have been close enough to hear the boy, and, you know, get excited and say he also saw them." Jack started preening. It helped him remember things.

Felix wrote down *vampires, legs, Clyde?.* He looked up, "Okay, keep going."

"She jumped off the skateboard, set one box down, and carried the other to the front door of your witness house, and knocked.

Then the blue jays showed up next door and started throwing out all the seed."

"Hnh." Felix wrote down, *one box delivered to witness #1, blue jays tossing contents of the birdfeeder across the street.* He wasn't convinced blue jays had anything to do with it. But, they were in the middle of one of their morning destructive bents. Better to write it down. "And then what happened?"

"Jake, the witness, answered the door. Took the box. She went back to her skateboard. And then that blue truck showed up. A man rolled down the window and waved at the girl and the boy. Said something I couldn't hear. She said, "Okay! I'll come straight home after this last box!" The boy said, "Spring's the worst for these things." I did hear one thing from the truck though. The man yelled something about vampires and eucalyptus."

Felix stuck his Thinking Straw back into his beak and wrote, *eucalyptus kills vampires?*

"Then the truck left. The girl left. The boy smacked his knee and grumbled something about dangits. Then he pushed the lawnmower back into the garage behind the house. The squirrels knocked down the birdfeeder across the street. My murder was on the ground eating and that's it."

"You left to fly across the street then?"

"Yup."

"That's good information. Thanks, Jack. Anything else you think I should put in my thinking notes for the considerations?"

"That neighbor across the street doesn't fill her feeder full enough."

"They never do, Jack. They never do."

Chapter Seven - *Digesting the Evidences*

Detective Felix breathed the sigh of reliefs. Perched on his digesting perch, he chewed slowly in deep thought. All the gathered evidences from Butters and Snickers lay before him. Photos of pistachios shells strewn throughout both alley crime scenes. Photos of trees, branches overhanging, shed doors (all closed seemingly locked), screen doors. Crime Scene Two's screen door was damaged. Crime Scene One was, alsotoo. Felix grabbed a pumpkin seed. He twirled it around in his beak with his tongue, thinking.

A photo caught his eye that lay with just it's corner exposed from under all the others. What he could see was strange, he pushed the top collection over to reveal the whole of it. Detective Felix let out a harrumph. It was just Clyde photobombing an evidence shot. His head was huge. Eyes blurred into a smear of raccoonery. Butters obviously had to deal with him the entire day.

Felix threw the photo on the floor. He had no time for shredding. He chewed while reading the report submitted by Snickers with regards to all other clues alongside the photographed evidence.

"Evidence was gathered and enumerated. Pistachio shells are contained in two crime scene bags. Under the couch. Noted details of investigationings:

Both crime scenes were stable and reflective of the environment and neighbor's thingys.

Both crime scenes contained the same count of pistachio shells."

Detective Felix stopped reading there. "Same count of shells ..." He spoke out loud to himself. Was that a setup? Was the criminal trying to throw him off the trails?

As if by universal proxy K9 Angus arrived sitting up straight. "Hi, boss! I have news about smells."

Detective Felix looked down, "Morning, K9 Angus. What do you have?"

"Well, I followed the scent of the clues to the criminal, like you said to do. First he was in the alley, then he went into a shed I couldn't go in but I could smell under the door. Then he walked to the other side and then I walked around the house. Then I lost the scent. THEN, I found it again at the other house and I walked around there, and then to the front and then to the shed I couldn't go in but I could smell under the door. And then he went to the front and then I lost the scent. It's like he disappeared."

Detective Felix detected a clue. "Or he went through the door. Why do you say, he?"

"Oh, yeah. Yup. Yes. He."

"How do you know?"

"Because boys smell funny. Not funny, ha ha, but funny, weirdo. Like if I found a boy, I wouldn't lick him."

"Are you sure about this?"

"Oh, yeah. Yup. Yes. I wouldn't lick him."

"No, I mean the boy part, the he part."

"Oh, yeah. Yup. Yes."

Before Detective Felix could ask another question, K9 Dante ran around the couch, jumped on K9 Angus, and snorfled his butt. They disappeared around the other side of the couch. With a crashing thud.

Felix heard *her* voice from the kitchen, "GUYS! Stop it or you're both going IN A BOX!"

Detective Felix added a note into the Snickers Report. *Possible boy subject. K9 Angus findings; smells funny.*

The Pistachio Alley Puzzle | A Detective Felix Mystery

Detective Felix's cellphone fartsounded. He dug it out of his Detective Coat hanging near his hanging Shredinator Toy, with his Detective Pocket nearest, at the ready.

"Detective Felix." He'd grabbed a new straw and stuck it in the corner of his beak. Thingys were heating up and K9 Dante was in a box. Which was a kennel big enough to hold a polar bear if you asked Detective Felix, but no one has, yet.

"Felix! I have information regarding the case." Leonidas thumped while he proclaimed his news. The blood of a fiery Furry Bureau of Investigationings Agent still thrummed in his veins.

"Morning Leo, which case of the two cases?" Felix needed precise information now.

"There's only one case, and there's a third crime scene just this morning." Leo let the news sink in, Felix's side of the line went silent. He chugged his carrot juice in anticipation. It wasn't every day he got ahead of a parrot. "Same alley, but another block down." He grinned while taking another drink. A bit of carrot juice slipped out the side of his grin leaving a trail of drops on his bunny furred shoulder. It was worth it.

"Are you at the Fast Through Pass Through?" He was going to need all hands on deck.

"Where else would I be? This is the nerve center for your information needs."

"I'll be there soon." Felix hung up and dropped his phone back into his Detective Pocket, then took the coat off the hangy thingy and threw his Detective Coat on. He lifted his collar up to keep the confused from getting in.

"Snickers! Butters! There's another crime scene to investigate!" Detective Felix called out into the Detective Agency, which *she* called a **birdroom** which was ***utterly ridiculous*** because *it was his detective agency location*!

"HUH?" Snickers was head first in his breakfast bowl.

"HI!" Butters was half asleep with her head in her breakfast bowl.

There is no fighting the way of the macaw. Which is why Felix thought of them as dactyls. Stubborn as flying dinosaurs, all of them. "Alright, fine. I'll get back to you with the location of the crime scene three."

Detective Felix headed out to the Fast Through Pass Through leaving his best team to finish breakfast like a pack of flying dinosaurs. You can't make a dactyl do anything a dactyl isn't ready to do.

Chapter Eight - *Blood Sucking Allergies*

Detective Felix found himself standing at the edge of the third crime scene. Pistachio shells as far as his eyes could see. The area was in the same alley, but the next block south. His eyes wandered from shed to shed zig-zagging focus revealing a scene he's seen twice before. Behind he heard the flutter and landing of two of his best from the Foragensics Team.

"Butters. Snickers. Ready to get to work?" He chewed his Thinking Straw, leaning back on his reverse talons.

"Yes, boss." Butters took off her lens cap, turned on her camera, and checked her IOS. She was going to need a fast shutter today.

"I'm ready and steady, boss. Went to bed early last night. I had a feeling things would get weirdo, today." Snickers went to bed early because he started trouble. No need to split hairs at a crime scene though.

Felix nodded toward the scene. "Have at it. When you've got it all, leave it at my digesting perch. I'm going backwardings to the other two crime scenes and see if I can see any other clues from the areas."

His foragensics pros were already past the edge and into the scene working. Butters placing numbered panels next to each shell. Snickers notating sheds, doors, prints, and thingys out of place. Detective Felix reminded himself to have K9 Angus scent the scene today. He headed to the first crime scene, one block north. It wasn't lost on him that the criminaling activities had backtracked north, then south of the original criminaling activity. He pulled out his Detective Notebook of Notes for Thinking, and The Pen. Jotting down questions he'd need answers to from the third scene. Felix looked up then down to write, keeping his notes and talons of fury straight.

A voice greeted his arrival. "There's the bird of the hour! What's the third scene look like?" Leonidas had caught up after begging a few extra minutes from Felix at the Diner. He couldn't just go gallivanting around without making sure Gary had it together for the lunch rush.

"Who's manning the helm at the Fast Through Pass Through? Did you leave Marie all alone to man handle grumpy lunch customers and grumbling ground squirrels?" Felix dropped the notebook and pen back into his Detective Pocket.

"The only grumpy customer is you." Leonidas laughed with a small rabbit foot thump. "She'll be fine with the general public and I worry more for the ground squirrels …here." Leo held out a white paper sack. "She was worried about your low blood sugars." Leo winked. Was that a nudge-nudge?

Detective Felix took the sack with a side glance avoiding the nudge-nudge of Leo. He unrolled the neatly folded over many times opening. "Ah! My regular plus sides. She's a peach." He tossed a pistachio up in the air and caught it in his open beak, careful to place the two empty shells back into the bag.

"She must have a thing for birds in uniform." Leonidas thoroughly enjoyed harassing Felix about Marie
.

"I wear a Detective Coat." Felix grabbed a pasta wheelie next. He bit off a section of tire to the wheel. He never ate the cog, just the tire and spokes.

"Maybe you're wearing a uniform in her dreams." Leonidas let out a rabbit giggle. A defining laugh that punctuated expertly delivered one-liners that never failed to ruffle the short feathers at the top of Felix's back.

"Weirdo." He snapped more wheel off the wheelie and crunched. "Did you join me just to harass my lunch snack attack?"

"I know you need by agency skills. One. And two, you've got three crime scenes. That's a bit much even for a detective like you. And I've got a bit of insider information for you that might zip up that third scene quickly."

"Hnh." Felix dropped the remaining wheelie into the bag and dug around to find a perfectly square chunk of cantaloupe. "Well, let's go find a spot for me to eat my snack attacks, and you to share insider information." They headed for an empty wood crate on it's side. A dark corner for a rabbit, a good place to lay out pumpkin seeds.

"I found a widow. She lives at crime scene three, but her husband traveled between one and two about the time frame of those crimes." Leo grabbed a yellow dandelion to eat while he waited for Felix to consider this idea.

"Widow? The husband just died?"

"Yeah. Severe nut allergic reaction. Dropped like a rock."

"Thanks for the visualizationings." Felix cracked the pumpkin seed in half to find the meat inside. "So, which house does she live in? Is she home?"

"She doesn't live in a house, but she is home." Leonidas grinned waiting for the "look". Felix's Eye of Surprise pleased Leonidas. Getting ahead of Felix was a prize in and of itself.

Felix turned his Eye of Surprise south, to watch Butters and Snickers work the third scene. He had a question. He pulled his cellphone out of his Detective Pocket and speed dialed Snickers. He watched Snickers answer his own cellphone.

Snickers was in the middle of writing down the shell count when his cellphone rang. *PEWPEW!* It was Detective Felix.

He balanced his notebook and pen in one wing and grabbed his cellphone from his Foragensics Fanny Pack. "Yeah, boss."

"Sorry to interrupt, I just have one question, if you know the answer."

"Sure."

"Have you got a full pistachio shell count, yet?"

Snickers knew Detective Felix was onto something. "112."

And together in criminal investigationings unison, Snickers and Detective Felix spoke into their phones, "The exact same count as the others."

"Thanks, Snickers." Felix disconnected the call and looked at Leonidas finishing the yellow flower of a dandelion. "We have one criminal. Three crime scenes. And one widow I need to talk to now."

Leo rubbed his paws together, smoothed his face fur, and pulled one ear one at a time, fussing with his appearance. "Well, let's go. She's waiting to talk to you. She wants justice."

"Don't we all, Leo. Don't we all."

Chapter Nine - *The Confused is in the Details*

Butters enjoyed her job. It provided her the lifestyle she preferred; quiet alone diva time. She didn't see herself as a diva, but wanting to be alone cast the shadow of diva. Not being a girl who worried about what others thought lent itself to ignoring that diva shadow.

She let her focus slide from the camera to Snickers on the other side of the crime scene. He was on the phone. She heard the ringtone, *PEWPEW!* Detective Felix must be onto something. She and Detective Felix were alike in the "ignoring what others think" department. They were different in the "talking on the cellphone" department. She appreciated him not calling her.

Butters looked back through her viewfinder, framing a cluster of pistachio shells and their numbered marker plate. She framed the crime scene ruler for the best presentation. *"Click"* She looked up to choose her next cluster shot. And worked her way towards Snickers.

She looked up to find a good scene context shot, and noticed a discarded cardboard box. Snickers hadn't set a marker plate next to it. Boys were not as sensitive to the strange and unusual as girls. She turned slightly to work her way toward the box rather than Snickers. *"Click"* She to the scene context shot from where she adjusted her direction forward. Context is everything when it came to the strange and unusual.

Detective Felix found himself back at the blue bucket, Leonidas leading the way. The bucket had been drained and turned upside down to keep rain waters from filling it up again. Leonidas jumped on top of the bucket and put both paws on the side of the shed, as if to start climbing. Rabbits do not climb.

"Where you going there, rabbit?" Felix pulled a new straw to chew on, out of his Detective Pocket. He grinned.

"I'm not going. I'm knocking. You need to get out more as a civilian, my friend." Leo didn't bother looking down to speak, he reached as far as his paws could go. "Mrs. Tic? Good morning!

Mrs. Tic! Are you there?" Leonidas hopped down to the ground. "Give her a sec. She's been through a lot."

Detective Felix raised one brow entertaining a friend who swerves toward the dramatic. "Oh, sure. I'm all soft gooey center Felixy, Leo." He pulled out his Detective Notebook of Notes for Thinking and The Pen. While waiting for the widow he wrote, *112 shells/60 pistachios* then, *180 pistachios ...???* He paused and quickly added, *nobody asked.*

His cellphone fartsounded. He answered quickly not wanting to have a phone call overlay a witness interview. "Detective Felix." He flipped his straw to the other side of his beak with his tongue.

"Boss. I got something over her at CS3." It was Butters. She never calls. She rarely answers. Must be important.

"Sit tight, Butters. I'm about to interview a witness near CS2. I'll be right over when I've got her statement in my Notebook thingy."

"Sounds good. Make sure to ask her if she has the other sock. And double check around there for a box that has blue words on the side that say, scout cookies." Then Butters was gone.

"Other sock? Scout cookies box?" He stood looking at his screensaver of R2D2 Droid flashing a recorded image of Princess Leia. He loved the Star Wars. Confused Clues come in all kinds of thingys. The screensaver proved Butters hung up first.

"Good Morning, Agent Leonidas. Detective Felix I presume."

Detective Felix wanted to take a picture of this moment for a new screensaver, but fought the impulse. "Mrs. Tic. I'm sorry for your loss."

Snickers was counting in his head out loud while pacing the length of Crime Scene 3. "19, 20, 21 ...twenty one feet. "Butters the CS3, CS2, and CS1 are all the same sized area! That's gotta mean something for Detective Felix." He wrote his findings down in his Foragensics Notebook of Foragensics Details.

Butters took her last photo of pistachio shell clusters. The cluster closest to Snickers. She'd taken a photo of the discarded scout cookies box. She would have liked to move it to get another photo of all the other words probably on the side hidden against the ground. But, Detective Felix preferred she not move things while doing her job. She stepped back and took a full crime scene photo for context and comparison. "For what it's worth, these pistachio clusters are familiar as well. They seem ...habitual. Did you notice that box over there?"

"I'll write that down for the detective. Yeah, I noticed the box." Snickers scribbled a few lines in his notes for their CS3 folder. "Where is Detective Felix, anyway?"

"Over there", she nodded toward Crime Scene 2. They could both see Leonidas and Felix standing near an upside down blue bucket while talking to the corner of a shed. "Did you add that box as a detail in your report?"

Snickers did not. But since he was currently jotting notes and could cover his oversight with appearing to be insightful, he lied. "I did. And I'm making additional notes about your thoughts on the matter of the scout cookies box." He drew a Universal Annoying Co-Worker Doodle next to the words *scout cookies box that probably isn't anything but Butters is making a big deal out of something not anything, as usual.* He then finished drawing the Universal Annoying Co-Worker Doodle which is just a darkly inked bunch of circles you draw really hard until the notebook paper indents from the weight of annoying and ink left behind. He drew an arrow from the doodle to the note about Butters being annoying.

"Thank you, Detective. That is a kindness." Mrs. Tic held her handkerchief to dab tears from her eyes.

"I'll try to keep this short, ma'am." Felix didn't want to watch a widow fall apart this morning.

"I will tell you everything I saw. Everything I heard. And everything my husband said before ...before ..." Mrs. Tic choked on the words. Her tears came quickly. But. She owed her husband her strength, now more than ever. They would have justice. She straightened, wiping the last tears away. "Before his untimely rupture."

Detective Felix pulled the straw from his beak. "Wait the minutes. Ma'am, I thought this was an allergic reactionings."

"HA!" She threw her antennae back cynically. "Of course that's what *he'd* LIKE you to think. How convenient. For *him*. Mr. Tic had no allergies. He was fit as a fiddler crab." Her appearance changed from defensive to proud. She looked down toward the Detective and Agent.

"I have no doubts, ma'am. I have just one more question. Do you know anything about a sock, or maybe a pair of socks? And possibly scout cookies?" He realized he'd just asked three questions. He waited, holding The Pen point to the notebook page, ready to take down the next big clue.

"OH! We're back to THAT AGAIN are we?" She rolled her eyes in disdain, tapping three of her six feet.

"Ma'am? *What* exactly, again? A sock. Two socks. A scout cookie box?" Felix started drawing the Universal Blah-Blah Case Notes Doodle. A tic-tac-toe board.

Leonidas grabbed another dandelion. This was going to take a snack attack minute.

Chapter Ten - *Wait the Minutes*

Leonidas and Detective Felix found themselves seated at the Fast Through Pass Through counter. Leonidas to Felix's left. Felix didn't like anyone messing around on the right. Because his Detective Pocket was over there.

Laid out in front of them on the counter, in no particular order, were all the photos, notes, evidences, and clues from three crime scenes. The totality of which covered enough counter space to force other patrons to seek barstools four stools away. Leo sipped carrot juice. Detective Felix drank his warm teas of delicious peaches.

"Fee, can I see your Detective Notebook of Notes for Thinking?" Leonidas wanted to see where Felix thought the clues were going.

Detective Felix reached into his Detective Pocket and pulled out his notebook and The Pen. He absently laid them in front of Agent Leonidas while shuffling through photos with his other wing. "Here. There's something annoying me about the shells. I can't put my talon on it, but it feels confused. And this scout cookies box. Two boxes one at CS1, and one at CS3. But none at CS2. Maybe we have the crime scene chronologicals in the disorders …"

"Hnh. I'll give it all a once over." Leo flipped pages up as he searched for the shell notes. Felix was a great note taker for a parrot. He was an awful note taker for a rabbit. Leo read slowly, trying to think like a parrot. He sipped carrot juice and read.

112 shells/60 pistachios" then, *180 pistachios …???* then, *nobody asked*

"What's this about nobody asked? Asked who?" Leo grabbed The Pen to add his notations. And to do some math. It was off.

"Nobody asked The Felix." Felix re-ordered the photos in a way that caught his attention. He stopped moving them to think. He was only slightly aware he'd answered a question. He was fully aware of the two photos of two discarded boxes being combined to make out all that was written on the boxes. Blue ink said girl scout cookies. Black ink from someone marking on the box that spelled out gibberish. Obviouslies written later. He focused on the blue ink.

"You expect a criminal committing a criminaling activity to ASK you first?" Leonidas drew a dark line through *"nobody asked"*. This was a note by a parrot thinking like a grey, not a detective. And this is why Leonidas left reading Felix's Detective Notebook as close to the end of evidence gathering as possible. He noticed the Universal Weirdo Doodle two pages before. Leonidas was surprised there was only one. Normally Detective Felix had a full page of Weirdo Doodles at this point in a case.

Detective Felix looked up taking in the question thrown out like yesterday's sweet potatoes. Sometimes Leonidas was way too much rabbit. So rabbity. "What criminaling activity do these pistachio shells have to do with? What are you talking about? Are you confused?" Felix took a long drink of his warm teas going cold waiting for his train of thought to come into the station.

"What criminaling? Felix!" Leo gestured to three crime scene's worth of evidence piled on his counter. Bags of pistachios shells. Photos. Notes. More notes. Evidence that was questionable. Evidence that was circumstantial. Evidence that was admissible. Evidence that was ...who put a sock in here? Leo tossed The Pen on top of the notebook that lay on top of a ream of evidences falling out of a folder labeled "CRIME STUFF". "Is this or is this not a crime? Why am I here?" He waited for an answer, paws crossed.

"Calm the downs bunny." Felix knew Leo did not like being called a bunny. But then Felix didn't like being called Polly. They knew each other's buttons. "Firstlies, we found a body. Mr. Tic. Secondlies, he is not a pistachio. D) If the body is not a pistachio, then pistachios are not clues. Er thego, there is no crime with pistachios!"

Leo threw his paws up, and then his face into them. "Why am I here, then?" He spoke the words through his bunny rabbit feet.

"You are hilarious. Which is good for me."

"Why did you have foragensics collect and count all the shells?"

"To find out if any were missing."

"Why did you do bad math in your notes?"

"So you would find it and ask."

"Why did you right *nobody asked* in your crime notebook?"

"Because nobody asked me if I wanted any pistachios! Which technicallying is a criminal activity. IF you ask The Felix! Which you did." Felix began gathering all the evidence into a stack. He tossed the three bags of pistachio shell evidence into the garbage can behind the counter. Shoved the errant short white sock into a folder marked "OTHER CRIME STUFF". He sat back on the stool and turned to look the best FBI Agent (retired) in the bunny face.

"We've still got a dead body. We still don't know who didn't ask me. We've got two empty girl scout cookies boxes. We don't know if those cookies taste good. And I for the ones, do not know what a girl scout *is*. And still, nobody knows if vampires are real."

"Where are you going with all that?" Leo sat back up. Felix was finishing sliding the paperwork and sock folder back into the "CRIME STUFF" folder.

"I'm dropping this off at my Tree Tent Office. And then I'm going back to the crime scene to see if I can find Clyde. And a skateboard. And one other sock. I'm pretty the sure I do not need to find the skateboard, though." Detective Felix closed the CRIME STUFF folder, wrapping the string around the button on the flap to keep it closed.

He hopped off the barstool and looked over his shoulder to Leo. "You coming or the what?"

Chapter Eleven - *Alleyways and Byways*

The alleyway running through the three blocks containing the three crime scenes has always been grass and weeds. This side of Mendota was the first to appear as the city came to life. And had yet to receive the city's concern for paving alleys. A hundred years on, their concerns had not changed. A tall grey house gave way to a two story white house to the south which gave way to a one story white house to the north. Home builders built out the block back and forth until they started new blocks on both sides. Crime Scene One is literally Mendota Scene One in the history of humans. No wilds or domestics care about human history. Because human history is the history of confused. Wilds and domestics keep track of things by keeping track of seasons and trees. A tree can tell you everything you need to know about before. Seasons tell you everything about before and what is coming. Alsotoo, none of that is confused.

Clyde had set up his world behind the house behind the alley behind Jake the Widower's, which is Detective Felix's ground zero Crime Scene One area of interest. Jake's two story red brick house and Ohio Buckeye Tree were the perfect go-to for raccoonery. But Clyde preferred housing on the other side of the alley. That human kept a rusty blue car parked outside along side the garage, it's front windows open. The front seat was filled with human cast off. Boxes, magazines, books, one stuffed bear that is now a mouse house and a dozen plastic jugs filled with air. Or, at least that's what they looked like to Clyde. But the backseat was perfect. Three blankets folded up and piled up. Perfect. For as long as Clyde could remember the backseat made the perfect resting spot. The mice would visit to take some stuffing from his blankets to repair and remodel their stuffed bear mouse house. But they were good neighbors. They only took what they needed for the season. He didn't mind.

The sun was coming up. The palest blue edged a pale yellow at the horizon. A single robin called a morning salute. No other robin's answered. It wasn't quite sunrise. Time to get to bed.

Clyde patted and folded his blankets into a fresh Clyde shape. He took the sock he found then filled with extra mouse house stuffing, patted and fluffed it. Stuffing stuck out of the end and he pushed it back in. What a great find. This sock made a perfect pillow. Better than the sock before.

Detective Felix found Butters and Snickers eating breakfast burrito bits at the corner near Crime Scene Two. He skipped breakfast at the Fast Through Pass Through to meet them early. The sun was just skimming the edge of the tree line about to burst into another day of investigationing.

"Good the mornings, team." Detective Felix stepped up to their breakfast nook of tree trunk and bush. His collar high and close to his neck keeping all potential confused out. A straw hung from his beak, the end in his mouth tattered and torn from thinking.

"Morning, boss." Butters, already done eating, was checking her camera for battery life and a clean lens.

"Monin, both!" Snickers was still chewing a mouth full. His beak covered in hummus. No more clues were needed about what they ate for breakfast.

"I shredded clues down to three items of the interests and two interviews." Felix was reading from his Detective Notebook of Notes for Thinking.

"So the pistachios didn't have any value to the investigation then?" Butters didn't look up from her camera.

"They proved nobody asked The Felix if he wanted any. Which technically is criminaling." Felix didn't look up from his notebook.

"What about the body?" Snickers had finished his breakfast and slipped on rubber investigationing gloves over his talons of inquiry.

"The body is a clue. But not one we are going to look at. I'm not doing any of that. Besides, the widow buried her husband yesterday. BUT, the cause of death is confused! Allergical reactionings or poisoning. The widow is sure it was diabolicaled."

"What am I looking for today, boss?" Snicker stood ready to head wherever Detective Felix pointed.

"A white sock." Felix flipped a page of his notebook. "Butters, I need photos of ...I need photos of ...lawnmower wheel tracks. And get K9 Angus to scent the trail of all the tracks you find. I need one sock. And proof there is only one lawnmower involved."

"One sock and one lawnmower?" Butters sounded skeptical. But Butters always sounded skeptical.

"One sock, one lawnmower, one criminal. And keep the Eye of Investigationings out for cookie crumbs." Felix flipped his notebook closed and looked up with a final nod of affirmationings.

Without another word spoken the three parted in directions serving their own purposes. Felix headed out to find Clyde. He heard a lawnmower start near Crime Scene Two. Chasing clues is confused. He and Leonidas had agreed long ago it was best to stick to the crime scenes and wait for the clues to show up. Felix ignored the lawnmower and headed toward a derelict blue rusty car with a raccoon asleep in the back. The same raccoon that was about to explode the lid off this case and he didn't even know it. Because he was asleep.

Detective Felix adjusted his collar against the confused he couldn't see. Pulled a new straw from his Detective Pocket for thinking while dropping his notebook and The Pen inside. A cat ran across the alley toward Clyde's car house. Jake's cat. With a bell and a pink collar of biter bug death dealing. He'd heard about that cat before. Jack said his name was Honey. Jack also said he hated that name, and that Honey could make enjoying birdfeeders a pain in the buttfeather.

Detective Felix stopped in his talon tracks, pulled notebook and The Pen out of his Detective Pocket and wrote, *biter bug death dealing cat?*, then dropped his note taking tools back into his pocket. He listened to the cat's collar bell disappear into the distance. His brain rang with fresh ideas, and stale clues.

His eyes stayed ahead of his talon steps searching for cookie crumbs. If there were girl scout cookies, and there were girl scouts, and scouts and girls were able to ask The Felix if he wanted a cookie but did not ...not a crime, but definetlies a criminaling activity. If you asked The Felix.

And right now, nobody asking The Felix a thingy.

Chapter Twelve - *That's Weirdo*

Tim followed the lawnmower's pace through the front yard. The new lawn mower was self-propelled. He just had to follow it while depressing a bar that ran across the length of the handlebar controls. With this much assistance from a lawnmower he could take more jobs.

At the property line he turned switchback to match the wheel path with the left front wheel. The cut path was greener, shorter and well mowed. He made sure to dress properly to keep bugs off his legs. That tick from the other day was too much, even for him. A grey blob of goo hanging on his sock. Just catching a ride. Already full. There isn't anything uglier than a bloated tick. Except two bloated ticks. He wore jeans, and his work boots today. "Nasty little vampires." He muttered out loud into the mower's constant whirling blade working to shave the tall grass.

He had flung that sock to the ground after he sat down to take a break. His cargo shorts were no help in hiding the sight of that thing hanging from the side of his team socks. His favorite ones, too. Basketball team colors, three colored rings around his calf proclaiming his fan status. And there between the first and second colored ring was that vampire barely hanging on. Creepy. Nasty. That thing was so close to latching onto his calf. Tim shivered with the thought. He yanked his sock off then and there and tossed it down. He put his Nike trainer back on and went home. Sockless on his right foot, hungry, and ready to be done with working and ticks. He hunted for his sock the next day. A dog must have grabbed it, or someone threw it away.

The constant hum and vibration of whirling blades allowed his mind to wander over the irrelevant things of life, toying at the strands of nothing important, as he entered the mowing zone. Buddha probably mowed to attain his nirvana.

"Clyde! Wake the ups, Clyde!" Felix perched on the open window of the rusty blue car looking at a pile of blankets. The blanket's slow up and down movements giving a clue. Clyde was in there sleeping.

The Pistachio Alley Puzzle | A Detective Felix Mystery

Raccoons do not snore. If you want to find a raccoon while he's asleep you better know where to look. Then look for the breathing. "Clyde Raccoon! Clyde ...hellos ...is your brain turned off? Wake the ups! I have investigationing questions. Hey, I gave up breakfast for you."

The blankets moved slightly, shifting, rising, rolling, tumbling back into the car seat revealing a raccoon hand, raccoon foot, and half a raccoon butt. "What time is it?" It's not morning tomorrow, is it?"

"No, it's not. It's still morning today. You went to bed early. You were supposed to wait for The Felix." Felix shifted talons of fury. "You should write these things down, Clyde."

Clyde bumped the blankets that were on top of him forcing the pile to fall off and back onto the rest of his nesting. He sat up while pulling his sock pillow around to set in his raccoon lap. It was warm. He wasn't going to let it get cold answering questions. "Okay, okay ..." He rubbed his face. He opened his sleepy eyes and looked at The Felix who's beak was wide open while his eyes stared at a raccoon's new pillow. "What?"

"Where did you get that!?"

"I told you the other day. Vampires. I found it in the grass over there by Crime Scene Two. I told you. There was a tick attached. I was going to hand him over to Paula Possum. She eats those things." Clyde felt a little tickle at the back of his throat. He was not going to throw up in his mouth in front of Felix. "So the tick says he's injured, and he needs help, and his name is Mr. Tic, and his wife is waiting for him at home. And can I take him there. Come to think about it, that tick did a lot of talking."

"What kind of injury!?" Felix pulled out his notebook and The Pen. The clues were gluing!

"If you ask me, he looked like he was about to rupture! Like a little tick volcano. I got him off the sock before he did. Then I walked him over to the shed and gave him to his wife to do whatever wife ticks do in that kind of situation."

"He ruptured." Felix wrote quickly.

"Well, I saw that coming."

"Did Mr. Tic say any things while he was with you?"

"He was rambling on about escaping a cat and poisonous biter bug collar shields. Something about that. He wasn't making much sense. He was already a goner. He talked about escaping a lawn mower by jumping on the white sock. That he almost didn't make it ...I told his wife all that. If you ask me, and she did, I think he tried feasting on that kid in the white socks. Got greedy, got stuck, and then got swatted. I heard that kid yell about vampires. I heard that."

"So you kept the sock for a pillow ..." Felix scribbled the Universal Doodle for gross thingys on a page in his notebook. A smiley face with it's mouth open and tongue hanging out with drips. "No signs of struggle on the sock?"

"WHAT? NO! Hang on now! I didn't steal this sock. I needed a new one to replace a shorter one that I used up. And this one, *WHICH I FOUND RESCUING A VICTIM,* has racing stripes. I fall asleep faster. I'm not sleeping on a crime scene or a stolen sock. His rupture must have happened at home. He was *ALMOST* rupturing when I found him. I didn't kill him, or steal a sock with racing stripes."

"You're not suspected of criminaling activities, Clyde." Felix flipped his notebook closed and dropped The Pen and notebook into his pocket. "You are a super cereal helpee helper witness, Clyde."

Felix turned to hop down off the car, but paused and turned around. "One more question, Clyde."

Clyde was already mostly under his blankets, only one Clyde foot and half a Clyde tail stuck out. His voice was muffled. "What?"

The Pistachio Alley Puzzle | A Detective Felix Mystery

"Were there pistachio shells already scattered around at that time? Do you remember?" Felix waited.

Clyde pushed up the pile of blankets to stick his head out. "Yes! Yes, there was!" I had walked through another pile at Crime Scene 1 before that. And now that you mention it, that kid and his lawn mower woke me up from there. Hey ...." Before Clyde could finish tossing off the blankets to finish his sentence, Felix had disappeared. "You're welcome!" He shouted in no particular direction then burrowed back under his blankets.

Felix sat next to Leonidas at the counter of the Fast Through Pass Through Diner. He sipped his warm teas of peach. Leonidas took a long draw of carrot juice. They sat in silence staring through the wide opening into the kitchen where his crew of ground squirrel short order cooks scrambled to get things ready for the breakfast rush.

"So, the clues glued up. The body belonged to a tick named Mr. Tic who left behind a wife, Mrs. Tic. Death due to a cat's pink Anti Tick Collar of death dealings. The pistachio shells were left behind by the lawn mowing kid taking a break from mowing lawns at three different houses. His finding a half dead half not yet ruptured tick on his sock was just a coincidence." Leonidas took another dreg of carrot juice.

"Technicallies we have to blame Jake the Widower for putting the death dealing collar on the cat. There is no such thing as a cat that puts on a collar on purpose. You can't tell cats what to do. "Felix nudged his tea cup deep in thoughts. "The cat was innocent bystandering. Alsotoo, the sock was happenstancing. And the body of the deceasered was buried by the widow, and she can do that, so that's not hiding the evidences. Jake the Widower murdered Mr. Tic. And Lawnmower kid didn't ask the Felix."

"Okay. Are vampires real?" Leonidas leaned on one elbow, paw under his jaw to look at Felix.

"It's the good questioning. We didn't find the evidence to prove any things about vampires. There could be vampires. I didn't find any thingy that says there are no vampires. But, you *can* technicallies call a tick a vampire. Like I call that one duck at my house a dick. Technicallies he is not a detective."

"Hnh." Leo nodded his head slightly, still resting against his paw. "I suppose that's not important to the case."

Felix sipped. "No it is the nots. We solved the murder. We solved the pistachios and The Felix not getting invited. If there are vampires it doesn't matter. Even if there are not vampires, he still didn't ask the Felix, any theway."

Leo sat up and pushed against the counter with both paws, stretching. "Well. What about the girl scout cookie boxes and the cookies?"

"That one was a tricky piece of the evidences. But I found a expert in the girl scout cookie informationings."

"Oh, yeah? Who's that?" Leo leaned forward resting his elbows back on the counter, he rolled his green bean to the other side of his mouth.

"Just someone who knows these thingys." Felix started stirring his tea. Felix never stirred his teas. He never stirred his tea cups when they were empty, either.

"Uh-Hnh …that's not an answer to a question, Detective. *BUT,* that is a body language that says a lot!" FBI training itched inside a bunny brain. "Spill the pistachios detective."

Their banter was interrupted by Marie coming out of the kitchen through swinging doors releasing good kitchen smells and shouting ground squirrel voices into the diner. She carried a tea pot. Without saying a word, she refilled the empty tea cup that Felix had been stirring and absently nudging.

She set the tea pot on the warmer under the counter in front of their stools. She popped her gum between her molars, and grinned. "Leonidas you're trying to pry two pieces of information out of one detective at the same time. That's not fair."

The Pistachio Alley Puzzle | A Detective Felix Mystery

She leaned her piggle paws against her edge of the counter top leaning in to create a private conversation of three like minds.

"Everyone knows Girl Scout cookies. Except you, Leo. There are no carrot cookies." She grinned more, her perfect guinea pig front teeth shined in the morning sun.

Felix continued to stir his now full tea cup. Not looking up, over, or under, for that matter. The potential for this to go the sideways was too big, even for a Felix.

"Also, you will never, ever, *E V E R*, find girl scout cookie crumbs. Anywhere. Ever. No one wastes a girl scout cookie." She stood straight and crossed her arms as best she could. Her arms were too short for real crossing. She crossed her guinea piggle wrists keeping her piggle elbows bent to look like a serious arm crossing.

Felix stopped stirring and looked up at her smiling face. "And no one ever, E V E R, shares their girl scout cookies. So there was no technicaled crime, or criminaling activities." He looked back down to stir more, but now smiling.

Leo jumped up from his stool. "OooKayyy …I do not want to know another thing about whatever this is right now. But as far as the case, that's that, right?"

"That's that." Felix sipped the last of his tea.

He held out his tea cup for a refill from Marie. She poured steaming peach flavors into his yellow tea cup. She glanced at Leonidas and asked, "Did you two hear the morning news?"

Leonidas was just about to walk away from his stool but dropped back down at her question. "What news?"

"There was a huge explosion at the phonebook factory." Marie looked over her eyeglasses and under her eyebrows. She snapped her gum between her back molars. "It's probably nothing but an accident." She nonchalantly spoke baited words over her shoulder as she walked back to the service counter

The Pistachio Alley Puzzle | A Detective Felix Mystery

facing their seats. She wiped her work area with a cloth. "I mean, who would want to explode phonebooks?" She grinned while looking through the wide opening into the kitchen. Ground squirrels zipped about in their business of cooking.

Felix pulled a new straw from his Detective Pocket and stuck it in his beak. Glad for the change of subject. And a question to answer.

Leonidas looked up to the ceiling pondering the question. "Hnh. That's a good question. Who would want to do that?" He looked down again, but found an empty seat where Detective Felix once sat. A yellow teacup, where a detective elbow once rested. Leonidas looked up to catch the sight of The Fast Through Pass Through glass front door close behind the best detective he knew, who stepped west toward a phonebook factory.

Marie followed his gaze and then looked at Leonidas. "Well, are you going or what?"

If you liked a good mystery by Felix you'll love a good laugh.

Best Sellers on Amazon!
ebook and print versions available

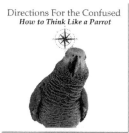

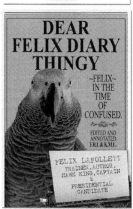

Coming soon:
*Detective Felix and
The Exploding Phonebook Factory Caper*

Made in the USA
Middletown, DE
28 October 2021